BELLA BUNHEAD

by Alessa Neeck

pictures by Lili Robins

Bella & Bruno Books
New York

For Gracie & Bruno

Library of Congress Control Number:
2013909345

ISBN: 978-0-9894402-0-2

My name is Bella and this is my dog, Bruno.

We have lots of friends who all have fun things they love to do. I wish I could find something I'm good at that makes me feel special too.

Annie points
her pretty feet
and flips midair.
It's such a treat!

Stephie draws
the clear blue sky
and paints a cloud
that passes by.

I sit and watch my friends and sigh,
and wonder, "Why, oh why can't I?"

Alexa sings a song so sweet
the birds all chirp,
"Tweet-tweet, tweet-tweet."

Christy writes her thoughts
in rhyme, then strums along
while keeping time.

Ashley laughs and smiles so bright, her spirit's captured day or night.

I try and try with all my might but see no answer there in sight.

Kate commands the stage so
coy and laughter fills
the room with joy.

Kara dreams of soccer fame.
She kicks the ball and wins
the game!

Amy threads her needle best, and sews a perfect princess dress.

Mara reads to her delight.
The pages turn and words
take flight.

The list goes on and on,
I think. Why can't I find
the missing link?

I cannot climb the tallest tree
or swim around so easily.

I cannot bake a scrumptious pie and certainly I cannot fly.

"What makes *me* like no one else?" I wonder, "Who am I?"

In my reflection all I see
are turned out feet and knobby knees.

I look myself straight up and down.
I check both sides and all around.

I start to twirl and whirl and spin,
and suddenly I start to grin.

I rummage through my chest of drawers
and find what I am looking for.

I swoop my hair up in a bun.
Now I'm really having fun!

My mind drifts back to ballet class.
"What made me just give up?" I ask.

The barre routine began just fine … pliés,
tendus, my time to shine!

But then things started getting tricky.
I couldn't dance the steps so quickly.

I got confused, all turned around,
and CRASH I fell right to the ground!

I didn't give myself a chance.
I stopped *believing* I could dance.

My friends succeed because they try.
"If they work hard, then so can I!"

With Bruno's help I stay on track.
Full steam ahead, no looking back.

I start to feel much more at ease.
I touch my toes, not just my knees!

And with each day that passes by
I practice with my head held high.

I pirouette with poise and grace,
and *now* I don't fall on my face!

I gave my all and tried my best. I'm glad I'm different from the rest.
At last I've found what makes me *me*, and happier I couldn't be.

"Bella Bunhead" my friends all shout.

"Yes, that's my name, don't wear it out!"

I hope you've had fun getting to know Bruno and me,
Bella Bunhead!

Just remember, as long as you believe in yourself
anything is possible. I found what makes *me* feel
special and so can *you*!

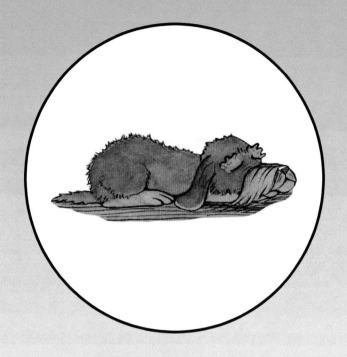

About the Author . . .

Alessa Neeck is a Broadway actress who lives in New York City. She started training as a ballerina at a young age, and quickly discovered her passion for the theater. She graduated with a BFA from the College-Conservatory of Music at the University of Cincinnati. Bella Bunhead was inspired by her multi-talented childhood friends, and is dedicated to her beloved doxies, Gracie and Bruno. This is her first children's book.

About the Illustrator . . .

Lili Robins graduated from George Washington University with a degree in fine arts and has been an illustrator and graphic designer for many years. Recently she has begun making pictures for children's books. She lives in Stafford, Virginia where she teaches yoga whenever she's not working in her home graphics studio.

LUCY!

36406765R00020

Made in the USA
Charleston, SC
02 December 2014